MR. HAnGRy
LOSES HIS SHIT

Roger Mee-Senseless

Mr Hangry was planning a dinner party. He didn't want to but had somehow got roped into a 'Come Dine With Me' style competition with some of the residents of MrandMrsLand and he was keen to land the thousand pound prize.

And so, he found himself in his local supermarket hungrily pushing around a trolley that was attempting to perform a complete 180 degree turn every time he touched it. This was item number 1 on the list of 500 things that Mr Hangry hated about shopping.

Number 24 was shopping while hungry and number 78 was 'people in general'. You see, Mr Hangry was not exactly what you'd call a people person. Although, he didn't get on with machines any better. He was currently having a stand up argument with the self-checkout (item number 251), which was repeating its favourite phrase 'unexpected item in the bagging area'. "How about if I drop my trousers and squeeze one out in the bagging area? Now that would be an unexpected item!" Mr Hangry screamed at the machine.

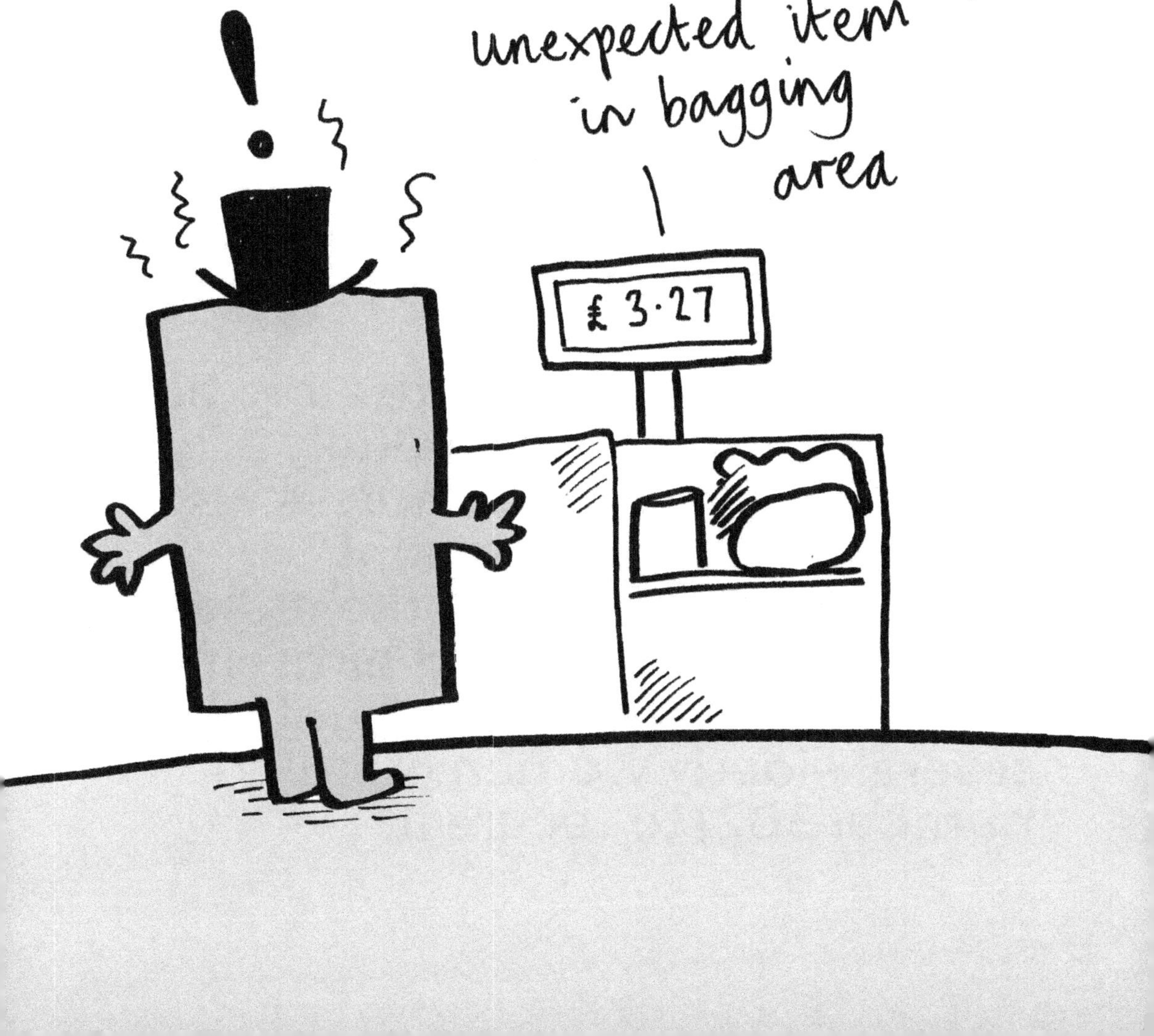
unexpected item in bagging area
£3·27

Mr Hangry was well known for doing this (shouting, not shitting on the till) and the supermarket staff simply let him vent rather than get involved.

Mr Hangry was also quite a big tight arse. So, rather than carefully designing a menu to impress his guests, he'd simply bought everything that was on the reduced shelf. He had impressed himself with his swiftness and had to fight off several elderly women (item number 302) to secure it.

He had bought: A loaf of bread (squashed), an overripe mango, some chives, some gravy and a pie that had been separated from it's box.

I'm sure I saw an episode of Ready, Steady, Cook in 1994 with these exact items, thought Mr Hangry. But I can't for the life of me remember what they made. Oh well, it was probably shit anyway.

Just then, Mr Hangry realised that he didn't know if anyone had any food allergies. Then he remembered that he didn't care.

He was pretty sure that all allergies were made up anyway. He didn't even know what gluten was.
It was probably a word invented by the media.

Leaving the shop, he ditched his trolley in the corner of the car park. As he pushed it, it started doing doughnuts all by itself, crashing into a brand new Bugatti in the process.

Mr Hangry walked over to the car and wrote the following note, which he left on the windscreen...

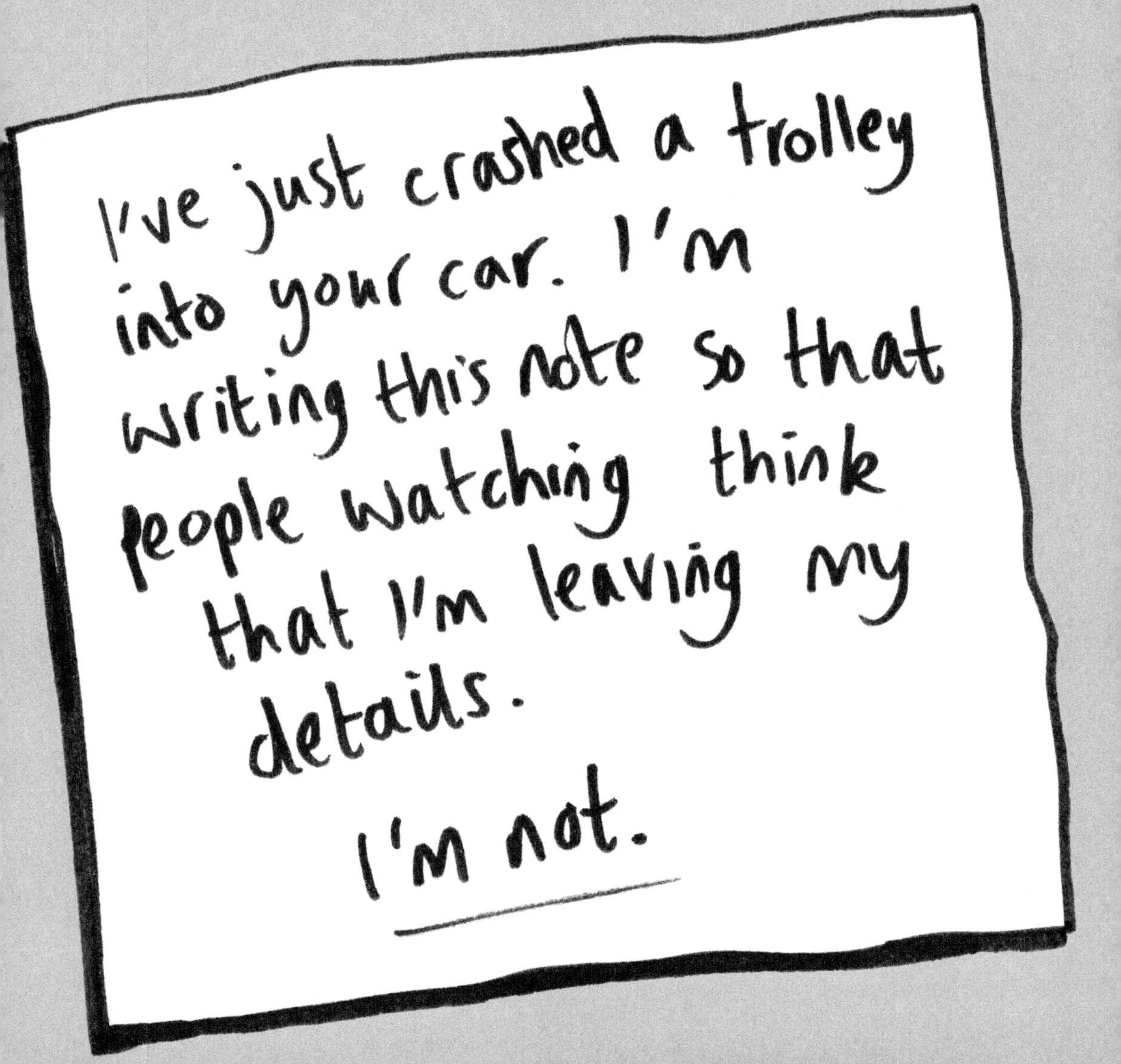
I've just crashed a trolley
into your car. I'm
writing this note so that
people watching think
that I'm leaving my
details.
I'm not.

He threw his shopping bag into the boot of his car and sped home, via the local park so he could shout at the children playing for no particular reason other than it just made him feel better.

Mr Hangry had another list of 500 things that annoyed him about driving.

Some of these were: people driving too fast, people driving too slow, people driving at exactly the speed limit, old people, young people, female and learner drivers.

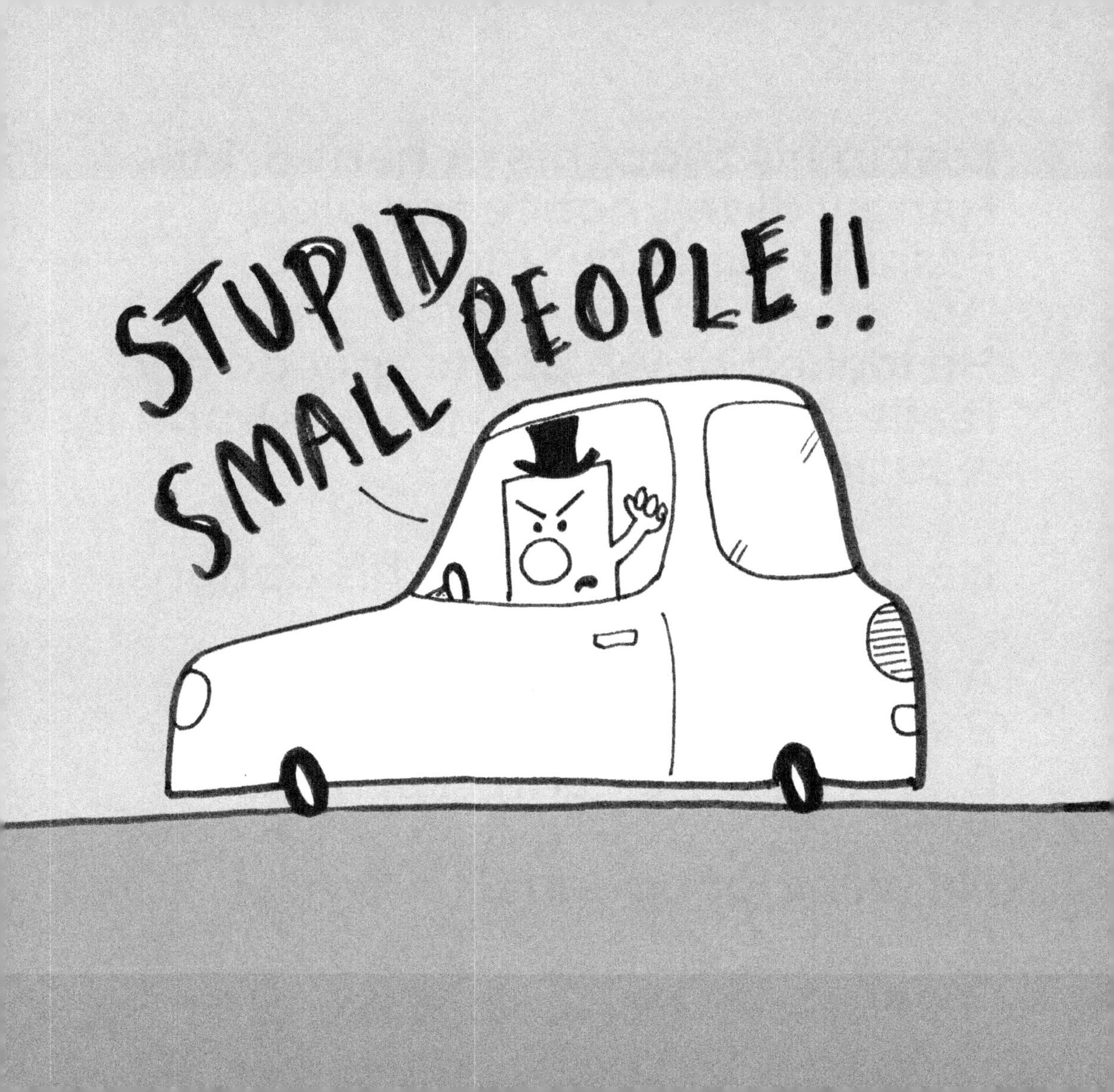
STUPID SMALL PEOPLE!!

Lost in his thoughts of hatred, Mr Hangry didn't notice the blue flashing lights behind him.

He looked down at the speedo and realised that he was doing 50mph in a 30 zone.

He quickly weighed up his options -

A - Pull over
B- Put his foot down
C - Pretend he hadn't seen them.

He went for option C.

After a couple of miles it was going to prove pretty difficult to say that he hadn't noticed them. Maybe I could get away with it by saying that I'm blind? he thought to himself.

Then he realised something - Mr Hangry lived in the rough part of MrandMrsLand. So rough that it was a no go area for the police. Sure enough, as he swung into his estate the police car siren died and it tailed off into the distance.

Phew, there are some benefits to living in a shithole, Mr Hangry thought.

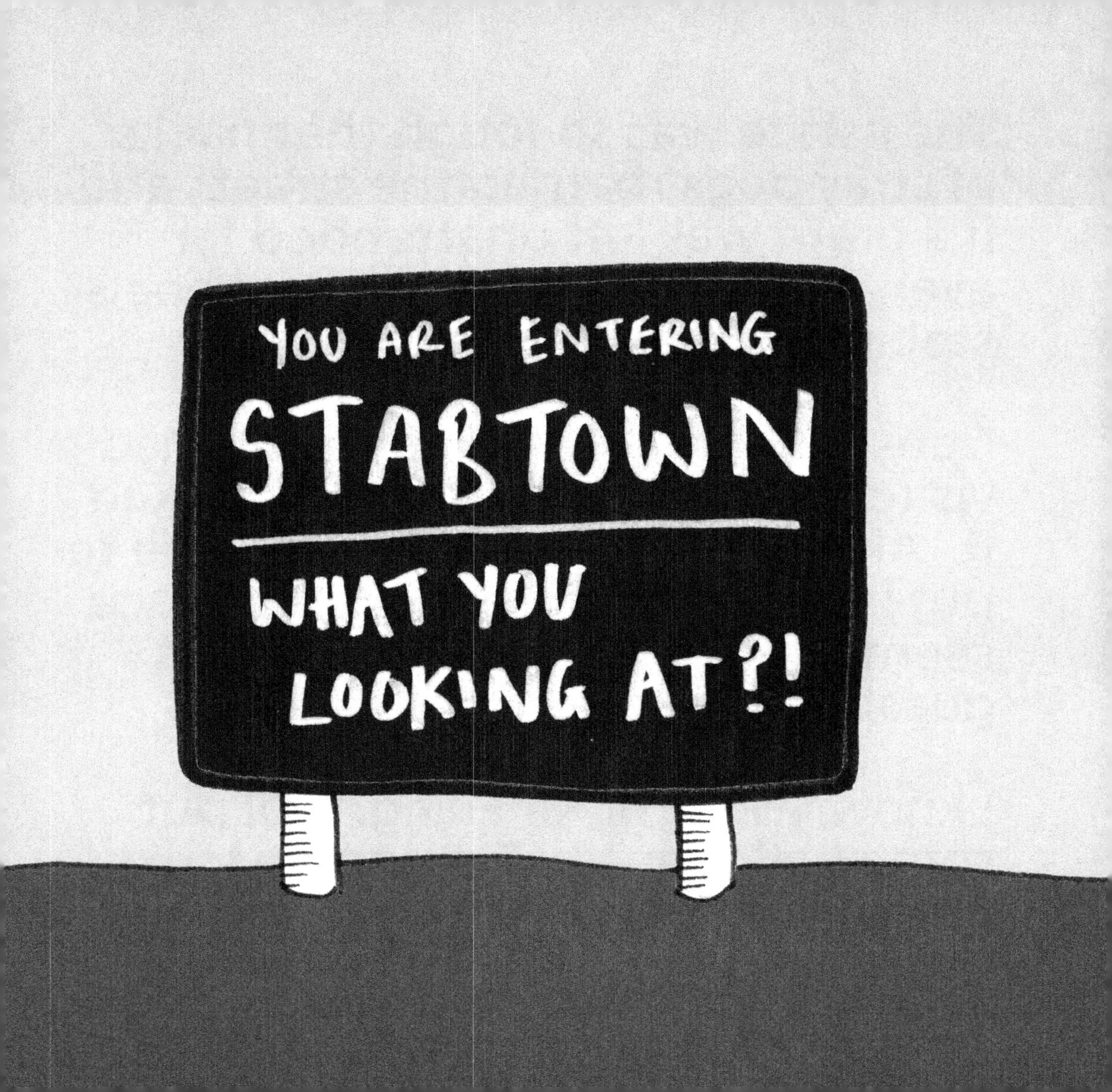
YOU ARE ENTERING
STABTOWN
WHAT YOU
LOOKING AT?!

The estate was so rough that packs of stray dogs roamed the streets and if a pram was left unattended for even a few minutes it had its wheels stolen and was left on bricks.

Consequently, Mr Hangry rarely had visitors, which was just how he liked it. Although, he was going to have to put in some effort to make his place seem a bit more appealing for his guests tonight.

I know, thought Mr Hangry. I'll put some balloons up. Everything looks better with balloons.

After he'd put the shopping away he sat down, switched the TV on and began to doze off to an episode of 'Celebs do Surgery'.

The basic premise of the programme was 10 'celebrities' are given a brief medical crash course and they are then allowed to perform non-emergency surgery on real patients. Their work was judged by Dr Dre and they achieved bonus points if their patients didn't die and weren't permanently maimed.

Today's episode featured Brummie heavy metaller, Ozzy Osbourne, attempting to perform a circumcision. Which, given his shaky hands, added a certain level of jeopardy to the situation.

When Mr Hangry awoke he realised that his guests were due in 10 minutes time. So, in a blind panic, he frantically ran a bath so that he could get himself ready. He ran the bath until there was about 2 inches of water in the bottom, which was just about enough to wash all the essential bits.

He was used to bathing in such shallow water as a means to cut costs on the water bill. And by the time he'd had a wee in it it'd be pretty full anyway. Washing his plates in the bath afterwards was another one of his money saving methods.

As he lay in the water he psyched himself up for the evening and resolved that he would try really, really, really, really, really hard to not tell anyone to fuck off, no matter how much they wound him up.

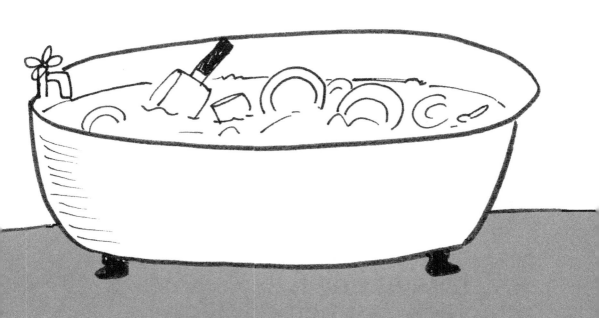

He'd even copied out a menu and stuck it to the door, such was his desire to impress his guests.

As the guests arrived, he quickly ran into problems.

He realised that he had got no idea how to cook the pie and, as there was no packaging, he just had to guess.

Mr Hangry served up the canapes which went down like a shit sandwich, not helped by the numerous pubic hairs that were found stuck to the plates.

Menu.

-Canapes-

cubes of freshly cut bread
soaked in gravy

-Starter-

chives served on toast

-Main-

Pie- I don't know what
flavour. You'll find out when you
eat it.

-Pudding-

mango served with a choice
of chives or gravy

The starters didn't go much better. In the stress of the situation, Mr Hangry had completely forgotten to check on the pie.

As he opened the oven door, the entire house filled with acrid smoke. The pie was cremated beyond recognition. Mr Hangry considered drowning it in thick gravy to cover it up but decided to just fess up.

"I've had enough," said Mr Salad Dodger. "I'm just going to order 20 pizzas, garlic bread, potato wedges and some ice cream for myself. Don't know what you guys want?"

"I'm happy whatever we have!" said Mr Happy

"Well, If I don't get the advertised food them I'm off," said Mr Uppity

"I DON'T MIND WHAT WE HAVE!" shouted Mr Noisy.

"Well if we have pizzas I don't want: pepperoni, onion, mushroom, chicken, peppers, pineapple, ham, anchovies, olives, egg, spinach, tomato or cheese," said Mr Fussy.

"I'm not sharing with anyone cus you're all knobheads, especially you Mr Happy!" said Mr Rude.

"Whatever we're doing can we please hurry the fuck up, I've got a train to catch in 3 minutes," said Mr Rush.

"I don't think I want a pizza, what if the delivery driver has an accident on the way here, it will be all our fault, I won't be able to live with myself." stammered Mr Worry.

"We can make our own pizzas out of old pairs of socks and human hair?" suggested Mr Nonsense.

"Yes, he's right," agreed Mr Wrong.

"I'll just have some of the leftover crusts," offered Mr Skinny

"We could just eat Mr Jelly?" suggested Mr Mean. "Has anyone got any ice cream?"

After extended discussions, an excel spreadsheet, several arguments, 2 fist fights and 3 people going home, the remaining Mr Men placed their order for their pizzas.

"I think if it's not here in the next 2 and a half minutes we should refuse to pay," said Mr Mean.

25 minutes later there was a knock at the door, Mr Clumsy went to pay and proceeded to drop them all over the floor. He tried to pick them up but fell over and mashed them further into the carpet.

"Oh great, who let that clumsy twat carry 20 pizzas?" stormed Mr Rude

Mr Sneeze went to help but had a sneezing attack spraying the pizzas with a thick layer of spit and saliva.

"I don't care, I'm eating them anyway, you lot are such a bunch of fuck ups!" said Mr Hangry.

AICHO
OOOO
OOO!

"Every time, something like this happens!"

Mr Hangry didn't win the competition, strangely.

Printed in Great Britain
by Amazon